Is It Christ

For Christmas Preparers everywhere.
Merry Christmas! Love Jane xx — J C

tiger tales

5 River Road, Suite 128, Wilton, CT 06897
Published in the United States 2013
Originally published in Great Britain 2013
by Little Tiger Press
Text and illustrations copyright © 2013 Jane Chapman
ISBN-13: 978-1-58925-149-6
ISBN-10: 1-58925-149-0
Printed in China
LTP/1400/0565/0613
1 3 5 7 9 10 8 6 4 2

For more insight and activities,
visit us at www.tigertalesbooks.com

mas Yet?

by Jane Chapman

tiger tales

"FASTER, RUDOLPH, FASTER!"

yelled Teddy, running around with his toys in his Santa hat.

"Watch out, Santa!" Big Bear grinned. "Your reindeer are out of control!"

"Christmas is coming! Hooray!" sang Teddy.

He just **COULD NOT WAIT**.

"Big Bear!"

"Yes?"

"Is it Christmas yet?"

"Not yet."

"Big Bear!"

"Yes?"

"Is it Christmas yet?"

"Soon . . . ."

"Big Bear!"

"WHAT?"

"Is it SOON NOW?"

"NO," growled Big Bear.

"We have to wrap all the presents, bake the cake, find the tree . . . ."

"I'll help!" beamed Teddy. "I'm a good wrapper-upper."

zzzzzzzzzzpft!

But wrapping was tricky . . .
and surprisingly sticky!

"Is it Christmas yet?" mumbled
a tangle of ribbons and paper.

"Almost," sighed Big Bear, "but we
still have to bake the cake . . . ."

"Ready, Teddy, cook!"
laughed Teddy with delight.

Big Bear popped the
cake in the oven.
"Is it ready yet?"
sang Teddy.

"NOT YET!" Big Bear
grumbled. "And it's not Christmas yet, either."

"**WHEN** will it be Christmas?"
moaned Teddy.
"**NOT YET**!" huffed Big Bear.
"We still need a Christmas tree . . . ."

"I **LOVE** Christmas trees!"
grinned the little bear. "Come on!"

The woods were sparkling with snow, as two busy bears searched for their tree. But Teddy was picky.

"TOO SPIKY...."

"TOO THIN...."

"TOO SMALL . . . ."

"This one is **PERFECT!**"

"Really . . . ?" mumbled Big Bear.

Big Bear and Teddy **HEAVED**…

and **HUFFED**…

and **PULLED**...

and **PUFFED**...

all . . .

the way . . .

home.

But the tree would not fit
through the front door . . .

or the back door.

And when they tried to pull it through the window . . .

SNAP!

"I DON'T BELIEVE IT!"

moaned Big Bear.

Teddy flopped down in a heap.

"OH, NOOOOOOOOO!" he wailed.

Big Bear gave his little bear an enormous Big Bear Hug.

"We can fix this," he whispered gently.

"Me and you. You're a great fixer-upper!"

"Oh, **YES**!" giggled Teddy.

Together, the bears taped up their
Christmas tree. Soon, they were
twirling tinsel and scattering stars!
   "Woo hoo!" cried Big Bear,
tossing the biggest star to the top.
   Teddy yawned. "Is . . . it . . .
nearly . . . ?"

zzzZZZZZZZZ

"Yes, Teddy," whispered Big Bear, carrying him up to bed. "It's very, very nearly . . ."

"CHRISTMAS!"